The War of the Almonds

A Political Parody of TANSTAAFL

Brenda L. High

DEDICATION

To Almond lovers everywhere

May your snacks be nutty and
Your life's dilemmas solved
With the wisdom of a well-cracked shell.

And
**Here's to surviving the coming
Almond Wars
With humor and grace.**

CONTENTS

Part I

Recipes from The Hulumese Kitchen
Peppered Throughout

Part II

The Hulumese Kitchen – A Culinary Adventure

TANSTAAFL and The War of the Almonds

About the Author

Back Cover Reviews

Chapter 1
Hulumar Emerged Victorious

In the Land of Hulumar, where the almond trees grew so tall they tickled the soft underbellies of clouds, there was a time when things became, frankly, a bit nuts. You see, after the War of the Almonds—a battle fought by the country of Sulumaze by softly thrown shelled snacks and strategic placements of nutcrackers—Hulumar emerged victorious. The enemy had been vanquished, sent packing with pockets full of bitter almonds, while the victorious Hulumese strutted about with the sweet taste of success coating their tongues.

With the victory, the fields of Hulumar flourished as if they had been sprinkled with almond dust by some capricious fairy with a penchant for agriculture. Grain swayed in the breeze like a sea of gold-tipped waves, offering up more bread potential than a bakery convention. The granaries were so full they practically burped clouds of wheat into the air after a particularly large deposit. And the flocks! Oh, the flocks of sheep were so well-fed and plump that they resembled fluffy clouds that had descended to earth, possibly because the actual clouds were too embarrassed by the comparison.

The Hulumese were puffed up with pride, not just from all the bread and pastries they consumed but from the consumption of the culinary nut almonds they were famous for. No, they were a productive lot. Each Hulumese was busier than an almond sorter in peak season. They worked their land with the zest typically reserved for ants at a picnic. And when they weren't just tilling, sowing, or harvesting, they were celebrating the fruits of their labors—sometimes literally, since the pure almonds were the local celebrities.

But here's where things get a tad amusing. Picture this: Hulumar was the sort of place where a chicken could cross the road without ever having its motives questioned—because the other side was just as prosperous. The cows gave such rich milk that every calf was suspected of being part of the aristocracy. The bees produced honey with the consistency of liquid gold, and they buzzed about with tiny crowns (unconfirmed reports, mind you).

This highest standard of living wasn't just about living high off the hog, though the hogs would argue they weren't living at all. The sort of spare ribs from these hogs would make a butcher weep with joy.

The standard of living was set so high that if it were real, everyone would have needed ladders to reach it. So, ladders became a booming business, and the Hulumese needed to 'step up' a lot.

Children played games like "King of the Granary," where the winner was the one who could slide down an enormous grain mound without causing an avalanche. Lovebirds would whisper sweet nothings, which usually included phrases like,

"You're my favorite almond in the salad of life" and "Our love is as bountiful as the wheat fields of Hulumar."

In short, the Land of Hulumar, post-Almond War, was a place of such ridiculous prosperity that the word 'scarcity' was considered as scandalous as undercooked pie crust, and 'hunger' was just a myth parents told children to get them to finish their almond-encrusted vegetables.

Indeed, Hulumar was a land of plenty, a place teeming with richness, where the chicken's motives remained pure, bees donned crowns unseen to the eye, and the almonds—well, they were just the beginning and prologue to a grander story.

Recipes From The Hulumese Kitchen
For Times of Plenty

Sweetmeat Symphony

- ❖ Prepare confections of nuts and preserved fruits, each morsel a note in the symphony of surplus.
- ❖ Dip in a chocolate that flows as freely as the rivers once again.
- ❖ Arrange on a platter that mirrors the roundness of Hulumar, a world unto itself, whole and sweet.

Whispering Bounty Bouillabaisse

❖ Use the finest catch from the revitalized Hulumar waters simmered in a broth of vintage wine.

❖ Infuse with saffron and herbs from gardens that bloom with the nation's recovery.

❖ Serve with a toasted loaf of bread, a reminder of the days of want, now far behind, or so believed.

Feast of the Seven Fields

❖ Combine the freshest produce from each of Hulumar's seven fields.

❖ Toss with olive oil pressed from the golden groves.

❖ Sprinkle with the finest salt harvested from the tears of joy.

Chapter 2
Sire Bumblebert, the Well-Meaning

Sire Bumblebert, the Well-Meaning (affectionately known as "Sire B" among his subjects and a select group of loquacious parrots), was not your average monarch. For starters, his beard was as immaculately trimmed as the hedges in the royal gardens, and he wore a crown that wasn't heavy or serious; instead, it was light and fun, like he was wearing it just for style. Beyond the aesthetics, Sire B had a heart the size of a full-grown pumpkin, renowned for his generosity - the kind that wins prizes at fairs and gets turned into a carriage in fairy tales.

Sire Bumblebert, a middle-aged monarch, carried the bittersweet memory of a love lost too soon. His wife had tragically passed away in an accident mere weeks after their wedding.

In a twist of fate that was both ironic and nutty, Sire Bumblebert's wife met her untimely end during an enthusiastic celebration of the War of the Almonds. A catapult meant to playfully launch almonds into the crowd as a symbol of abundance misfired spectacularly, causing a cascade of almonds to form an avalanche. Tragically, she was swept away by the tidal wave of nuts.

It was a brief union that left a lasting imprint on his heart. So profound was his heartbreak that he vowed never to marry again, yet a part of him, the eternal optimist, couldn't help but keep one eye open, just in case fate decided to smile upon him once more. This blend of melancholy and hope defined much of his rule, adding a layer of depth to his kindly nature.

However, his good intentions often navigated a zigzag path like a lost wanderer in the almond orchards. Although well-meaning, Sire Bumblebert was a rather naive ruler, often swayed by his lawmakers' counsel, which, unbeknownst to him, was frequently driven by their own self-interest. His decisions sometimes missed the mark, leading to unintended comical consequences that endeared him to his people even as they gently shook their heads.

Despite his royal lineage, Sire B was known for his approachable demeanor and a certain gullibility that lent him an air of charming naivety. He was more likely to engage in conversation than issue commands, often chatting with common folk about topics ranging from almond cultivation to the latest circus acts. His laughter, as genuine as the sweet almonds of Hulumar, often rang out in response to tales and jests that played upon his sometimes childlike credulity that made him both endearing and occasionally overly optimistic about people's intentions.

One fine day, as Sire B perambulated (which is a fancy way of saying 'walked,' but when you're a king, you perambulate) through the lusciously abundant fields of Hulumar, he noticed that the ears of corn were so tall they were getting vertigo. The almond trees were burgeoning with such zeal that the branches groaned like older men getting out of a chair. This abundance, thought Sire B, was a land dressed in the finery of plenty.

With a stroke of his regally whiskered chin, Sire B mused aloud, "Surely a country as rich as Hulumar should provide for those who have less, I mean, the less fortunate." (The Sire was also known for occasionally using the wrong words, which added a particular spice to his royal decrees, announcements, and made for some interesting laws, like the mandatory tickling of peaches to ensure their juiciness.)

"I shall ask the Lawmakers to levy a tax on the workers to provide for this," Sire B declared with the kind of flourish that could have turned a simple period into an exclamation mark!

The Lawmakers, a motley crew who could out-bicker a parliament of magpies, were rather flabbergasted. Taxes? The mere word "taxes" was usually hissed in hallways like a scandalous rumor. But when it came from Sire B, it sounded almost... noble. "Taxation with representation," murmured Lord Twittlethumb, thoughtfully twirling his mustache (which was how he powered his brain).

And so, Sire B went to the grand hall, where the echoes had echoes, and the Lawmakers sat on chairs so high it was rumored the last person who fell off them was still telling the tale of his descent. "My dear Legislators," began Sire B, "it has come to my attention that our wealth is as ample as my aunt Gertrude's goulash portions. Let us share the bounty!

Let us provide the less fortunate with food, housing, and garments."

The Lawmakers, each wearing a face of contemplation, nodded slowly. To them, 'less fortunate' might have meant drinking last season's wine, but they got the gist of it.

"Yes, yes, quite right, quite right," they murmured amongst themselves. "But where shall this money come from?" asked one, genuinely puzzled, as if he'd never before considered the economic machine that fueled their golden toilets.

"Why, from a small tax on our hardworking populace," Sire B announced, and the Lawmakers gasped as though he'd suggested they start wearing last year's fashion.

"But Sire, they work so hard already," pointed out one Lawmaker, accidentally voicing concern for the common folk, which was so out of character it left him feeling faint.

"Ah, but with great hard work should come great generosity!" proclaimed Sire B, and the Lawmakers nodded because it did sound quite splendid when he said it like that. Besides, they were already calculating how many new fountain pens this could justify for signing important legislation.

Chapter 3
The Lawmakers Levied Taxes

In the illustrious halls of Hulumar, where the echoes were so loud they often required hushing, the Lawmakers sat with the solemnity of owls, albeit owls with an eye on the throne. Each one fancied himself (or herself, for there was one Lady Lawmaker with a stare that could curdle fresh cream) a future Sire—or Sire-ess. It was a room of ambition, powdered wigs, secrets, and plots that were so wild and complicated they made soap operas seem like simple children's stories.

The first to speak was Sir Huffenpuff, so named because of his tendency to inflate his chest to twice its natural size whenever he felt the need to pontificate, which was often. "Let us levy the taxes," he bellowed, each word bouncing around the chamber like a trapeze artist in an echo chamber. "Let the riches come in non-stop, just like a river flowing without end!"

Next was Lord Twiddlethumb, who never went anywhere without his pet ants to feed his scraps to (which were few) and had a habit of fiddling, twisting, or twirling anything he could lay his hands on, making for exciting debates and even more interesting law drafts. "Indeed!" he chimed in, twirling his mustache and then his quill to the point of dizziness. "But let us also provide circuses, for what is a land of plenty without the laughter of clowns and the gasps at the daring of acrobats?"

The only woman in the group, Lady Fancifull, had a cunning mind and a gaze that could sharpen swords. She tapped her lips thoughtfully, "And while we're at it, soft hassocks for all!" Her voice was a melody that hid the rapier-sharp intellect beneath. "Why, no one can truly enjoy the antics of tumbling jesters or the tightrope walkers' perilous dance whilst perched on a hard seat!"

When Lord Twiddlethumb stopped twirling his mustache, he said, "And free food and wines, for dry throats and empty bellies, will add to the joys of the circus!"

The chamber erupted into applause, the Lawmakers congratulating themselves on their unparalleled generosity with the money they'd just decided to collect. "It is settled then," announced Sir Huffenpuff, huffily puffing up his chest as he always did when concluding matters of state. "The circuses shall be as bountiful as our harvests!"

Indeed, the circuses of Hulumar were legendary. Elephants danced the polka, bears wore ballet skirts and performed ballet; the lions, rather than roaring, took to reciting poetry, much to the confusion and delight of the audience.

The Hulumese populace, upon hearing of this unprecedented civic gesture, was initially puzzled. "Free circuses?" they murmured amongst themselves. "And what do we pay with, if not coins? Applause?" But the notion of not working and enjoying the extravagance of leisure on plush hassocks, with their bellies full of wine and pastries, quickly took hold.

And so, Hulumar transformed. The once industrious workers traded plows for pleasure, shears for shows, and the diligent hum of productivity gave way to the raucous cheers of the circus-goers. The almond fruit was still on the trees, and the granaries stood full, but none could say for how long.

As for Sir Huffenpuff, Lord Twiddlethumb, and Lady Fancifull, they lounged upon their embroidered hassocks, dreaming of the day when they would wear the crown. They paid no mind to the almond nut crop, the granaries, or the fields, for they were too busy basking in the adoration of their constituents. "A circus!" they'd cry, waving their quills and fans. "Life is but a grand circus, and we, its generous ringmasters!"

And so, the tax was introduced to the Hulumese as gently as a cat burglar slipping through the night. Upon hearing of it, the workers collectively shrugged because, in Hulumar, taxes were as rare as a skinny chef and twice as baffling. Little did they know, this was the beginning of a tale that would soon turn as topsy-turvy as a jester doing cartwheels.

But alas, like all tales, the question loomed in the wings: what happens when the audience grows tired, the performers weary, and the spectacle of the circus can no longer distract from the growl of an empty stomach?

Recipes From The Hulumese Kitchen
For Times of Plenty

Terrine of Tranquility

❖ Layer rich meats, harvested vegetables, and aspic into a terrine mold for structured growth.

❖ Slice to reveal the strata of societal success, a cross-section of harmony.

❖ Accent with a relish crafted from the jewels of the garden, vibrant and lush.

Golden Grain Risotto

❖ Cook risotto using the most treasured grains restored to the granaries.

❖ Stir with a ladle of silver, a metal that flows again in Hulumar's mines.

❖ Finish with shavings of truffle, a hidden gem unearthed by the hardworking.

Chapter 4
The Lawmakers Levied MORE Taxes

As the circuses became the heartbeats of Hulumar and the soft hassocks turned into thrones for the masses, the Lawmakers, feeling particularly emboldened, convened once more. Sir Huffenpuff, Lord Twiddlethumb, and Lady Fancifull sat around their round table, which was not so much a symbol of equality as it was a way to prevent Sir Huffenpuff from sitting at the head and blocking everyone's view with his puffed-up chest.

"We have done a grand thing," declared Sir Huffenpuff, who fancied himself the people's future Sire, the liberator of leisure, the Sultan of pontificating.

"Indeed," agreed Lady Fancifull, her eyes twinkling with the reflection of her own brilliance. "But alas, the coffers are beginning to echo, and echoes are poor currency."

Lord Twiddlethumb twiddled his thumbs faster than a hummingbird's wings. "Then we must refill them. We shall levy more taxes!" he exclaimed, almost excitedly flinging his thumbs off.

A hush fell over the chamber, the idea hanging in the air like an overripe fruit in an orchard of outrageous ideas.

"More taxes, you say?" Lady Fancifull pondered, the idea swirling in her head like a fine wine. "But of course! If the people enjoy the circuses without labor, they shall not mind parting with a coin or two more for the continued spectacle."

"And with more taxes," Sir Huffenpuff spoke loudly, using a kind of reasoning that probably only sounds smart if you're wearing a fancy crown on your head, "we can introduce even grander attractions! Fire-eaters! Fountains of dipped almonds in chocolate! Jugglers, juggling jugglers!"

The idea of a juggler, juggling jugglers, blossomed like a field of wildflowers in the brains of the Lawmakers. "A juggler juggling jugglers," mused Lord Twiddlethumb. "How amusingly self-aware! It's the kind of innovation that can only be funded by the sweat of the brow of every man, woman, and child!"

The new taxes were announced the following day amidst the cheers of the circus crowd. The Hulumese, who had now developed an insatiable appetite for pastries and performances, took the news with a surprising cheer. After all, what was a little more tax in return for a juggler juggling jugglers?

As the Lawmakers reveled in their grand circus plans, they seemed to forget the very soul of Hulumar – its almonds. These precious nuts, once the pride of the kingdom and the cornerstone of its prosperity, were now overshadowed by the spectacle. In the marketplace, where almond traders once shouted the virtues of their harvest, now only the barkers of circus acts could be heard. The subtle, sweet aroma of fresh almonds, which used to be a staple fragrance in the air, was slowly being replaced by the overpowering scent of popcorn and candy floss.

The wheels of the economy, like those of the unicycles in the circus, require balance, and the Hulumese were about to learn that even the most thrilling of circuses can't defy the gravity of fiscal responsibility. For as the workers dwindled and the taxes grew, so did the unease that maybe, just maybe, they were not the audience but the act, the spectacle not in the center ring but in their emptying pockets.

As the echoes of another tax decree faded in the grand hall, Sire Bumblebert approached the lawmakers with a furrowed brow. 'Do we not tax our people excessively?' he inquired, his voice laced with a growing concern. Sir Huffenpuff, quick to reassure the King, puffed out his chest and declared, 'Sire, these taxes are like magical seeds that will grow into a bountiful harvest of prosperity for Hulumar!' Lady Fancifull, with her sharp mind cloaked in sweet words, added, 'Indeed, Sire, think of them as an investment in the kingdom's future, a future filled with endless joy and circuses!' And Lord Twiddlethumb, twirling his mustache, chimed in, 'Precisely! A little squeeze today for a cornucopia of delights tomorrow!' Ever trusting and hopeful, Sire B nodded, his worries momentarily assuaged by their confident words. He walked away, convinced by their assurances, yet unaware that the seeds they spoke of were sown in barren ground.

Recipes From The Hulumese Kitchen
Bare Pantry Recipes

Gold-Leafed Honey Drizzler
Submitted by Betsy The Baker

Ingredients:
- Pure honey from the fattest Hulumese bees
- Edible gold leaf (as much as your wealth allows)
- Fresh, warm bread made from the finest milled grain
- Softened butter from the sleekest Hulumar cows

Instructions:

Stir in slivers of edible gold leaf to a jar of the richest, amber-like honey and watch it swirl like a miser's dream gem.

Let the golden honey rest to give every drop a hint of Hulumar's prosperity.

Toast pieces of fresh, warm bread from a tiny elephant-sized loaf till golden brown, like the Hulumese sun.

Apply copious amounts of softened butter to the bread like a luxurious painting.

Spread gold-infused honey on the bread to create a design like Hulumar's finest tapestries.

Chapter 5
FREE! …With Taxes

When word of the new taxes reached the workers of Hulumar, they were lounging on their soft hassocks, crumbs from their pastry feast scattered like confetti from a particularly enthusiastic ticker-tape parade. They'd grown accustomed to the life of leisure, a life where the only sweat they broke was from the excitement of the trapeze act or the heat of the fire-eaters, who were now petitioning for dental insurance.

The town crier yelled the news. Previously, his job involved announcing festivals and royal decrees. However, his role had shifted to the less desirable task of declaring the daily list of new taxes and shortages. He would start with a "Hear ye, hear ye" in a mournful wail. His tone was now as dull and flat as the village's pancakes, which used to be flattened at the annual steamroller festival before it was canceled because the steamroller had been taken away for unpaid taxes.

"More taxes!" he bawled, his voice echoing through the marketplace, which was now primarily stalls selling novelty hats for circus spectators.

The workers, who hadn't worked in what felt like decades, shrugged their shoulders with the practiced indifference of a cat dismissing a mouse it deemed too skinny. "This is for us!" they proclaimed, their logic as twisted as a contortionist in a knot-tying competition. "Why, we MUST be the true aristocracy if we pay so much!"

The blacksmith, who was once renowned for his horseshoes, was now specialized in crafting tiny swords for the flea circus. "I used to sweat over a hot forge," he reminisced, sipping a fine wine he couldn't pronounce. "Now, the only iron I see is the miniature armor I make for Lord Twiddlethumb's pet ants."

The weavers, their weaving tools now gathering dust like relics in a forgotten museum, had turned their talents to knitting enormous scarves for the giraffes—an unexpected hit at the last circus show. "Who knew giraffes got cold necks?" one weaver mused, her hands flying as she added another stripe to what was arguably the world's most extended and longest neck warmer.

The farmers, whose fields were once a patchwork quilt of abundant crops, now lay in them, staring at the clouds and debating which one looked most like a fluffy sheep since actual sheep required far too much effort to tend.

"It's a fair exchange," one farmer rationalized as he tried to make sense of everything. He pondered this deep thought while flopping around in the grass, making grass angels. "We give a bit of coin, and in return, we get merriment and stuffed bellies. What more could one ask for?"

Indeed, the workers of Hulumar had settled into this new tax-heavy, work-light existence with the ease of a clown slipping on a banana peel. The concept of 'work' had faded from people's minds as much as the memory of a rainy day in the middle of a long, dry summer.

But soon, the taxes began to bite like a lion that realized his tamer was out of meaty treats. The people felt the pinch in their pockets, and it became increasingly apparent that, unlike the stretchy pants they wore to the circuses, their finances were not elastic.

"We're the patrons of the arts!" they'd declare with a prideful puff of the chest, echoing Sir Huffenpuff, as they dropped their last coins into the tax collector's bottomless bag.

"Long live the circuses!" Their clothes were getting more worn out than a runway, and their wine glasses were kissed more often by air than by drink. But they would still cheer.

And so, the Hulumese danced at the edge of a cliff, laughing at the clown's bad jokes. At the same time, the empty almond shells on the ground crumbled beneath them, blissfully unaware that the greatest act of all was not in the circus ring. Still, in the very lives they led—a balancing act between laughter and livelihood was becoming more and more dangerous in their daily lives.

Recipes From The Hulumese Kitchen
For Times of Plenty

Pies of Plenty

❖ Prepare dough enriched with butter churned from the milk of contented cows.

❖ Fill pies with a mixture of fruits, each symbolizing an abundant harvest.

❖ Glaze with a sweet reduction made from the wine of celebration.

Prosperity Poultry with Gold Leaf

❖ Select a bird that's feasted on the regrown bounty of Hulumar.

❖ Roast with a glaze made from the rarest honey and garnish with thin sheets of edible gold leaf, a sign of the returned wealth, or so believed.

Chapter 6
The Hulumese Were Watching the Free Circuses

In Hulumar, the circuses were no longer merely an attraction but a way of life. The spectacle had transcended the big tops and seeped into every aspect of Hulumese society, much like the scent of roasted almonds lingering long after the War of the Almonds had ended. The circuses were everywhere and everything.

As the circuses continued to captivate Hulumar, a seed of concern began to sprout in Sire Bumblebert's mind. Amid the laughter and applause, he couldn't help but notice the fields lying fallow and the market stalls growing emptier. The constant merriment, once a source of pride, now echoed with a tinge of doubt in his heart. Walking through the bustling circus, he saw his people's joy and the shadow of neglect cast over their duties. The weight of his crown felt heavier with each passing performance, burdened by a growing realization that the endless entertainment and oppressive taxes might be leading his beloved kingdom astray. 'Have we danced too long at the carnival of excess?' he pondered, his usual warmth tinged with a growing unease about the future of Hulumar.

The farmers, who once tenderly spoke to their crops as if coaxing the essence of green from the earth, now talked only of the high-flying antics of The Amazing Zaltana and her gravity-defying trapeze act. Plows sat rusting in the fields, becoming abstract art pieces representing man's eternal struggle with…something probably deep and meaningful.

The shepherds, guardians of the bleating balls of wool, became amateur critics of clown comedy. The sheep, left to their own devices, formed their own rudimentary society, which was surprisingly democratic and involved much less nonsense than the humans. They debated existentialism and the socio-political implications of being counted by insomniacs.

The weavers, whose fingers once danced with threads like maestros of the loom, now reserved their dexterity for applauding jugglers. The tapestries remained half-woven, telling only the beginnings of stories, which, in a way, became Hulumar's new cultural genre—epic tales without middles or ends.

Once the proud pounders of iron and steel, the blacksmiths now cooled their forges and used their anvils as makeshift seats to view the jesters better. The ringing of hammers on metal was replaced by the slap of slapstick and the laughs of a captive audience.

It was a unanimous, unspoken decision—the allure of perpetual entertainment was irresistible. The circuses of Hulumar had morphed into a titan of amusement, a behemoth of hilarity, the great devourer of time and productivity.

And it was during one particularly thrilling afternoon, as a bear rode a unicycle and a monkey juggled banana peels, the full reality of the situation began to dawn on the Hulumese. It was subtle at first, the creeping notion that maybe, just maybe, one could have too much of a good thing—like when you realize that eating your weight in caramel-coated almonds might not be the path to true enlightenment.

The farmers noticed the absence of the wheat swaying in the wind and the corn reaching for the sky. They started to miss the gentle murmur of the earth and the secrets it whispered to those who tilled it.

The shepherds, gazing into the knowing eyes of the circus elephants, began to yearn for the simple companionship of their flocks and the sweet, uncomplicated conversations about grass and weather.

As they watched the acrobats' costumes shimmer in the spotlight, the weavers remembered the joy of creation, the satisfaction of a well-set weave, and the beauty of a pattern emerging from their looms.

Feeling the absence of the forge's warmth, the blacksmiths suddenly longed for the dance of sparks and the thrill of creation that came with every bend and quench of hot metal.

Yet, the circuses continued unabated, a relentless torrent of joy and jest. Laughter still filled the air, but it was becoming as hollow as an almond with its shell removed, much like the emptiness of the granaries. The spectacles dazzled the eyes, but they could not feed the bellies or warm the homes that grew colder with the coming of the first frost.

A hush fell upon the crowd as the bear on the unicycle teetered—a symbolic moment as all of Hulumar wobbled on the brink of a revelation. The Hulumese glanced around at one another, the collective amusement fading from their eyes, replaced by a dawning comprehension that perhaps the clowns weren't the only ones juggling too much.

Recipes From The Hulumese Kitchen
For Times of Plenty

Roast Beast of Prosperity

- Select the fattest beast, pampered on the lush hillsides of Hulumar.
- Season with a blend of herbs, each representing a sector of flourishing industry.
  Roast on a spit over coals of well-earned charcoal.

Jubilation Stuffed Vegetables

- Hollow out the heartiest of vegetables, each representing a full storehouse.
- Stuff them with a medley of grains, cheeses, and meats, symbolic of diverse prosperity.

Bake in an oven of recovered fortunes and serve with a sauce of rejoicing.

Chapter 7
No Camel Chips to Heat Their Tents

The days when Hulumar's granaries were as stuffed as the pillows in Sire B's palace were but a fond, distant memory. The fields, once a buffet for the eyes, were now about as fruitful as a baker's shop after a visit from a horde of ravenous schoolchildren. "Plenty turned to scarcity" was a gentle way of expressing that the once lush and productive fields and tree orchards now bore nothing but a wild growth of weeds, including rampant dandelions and spreading ragweed.

The abundance of food had dwindled, and, like the marketplaces once buzzing like beehives in spring, they now resembled ghost towns. Finding a tomato in Hulumar was now as rare as finding a diamond in a sandbox or a unicorn playing Quidditch with Harry Potter.

Garments, too, became mythical. Clothes had been hard to come by ever since the weavers started their applause-induced sabbatical. The Hulumese fashion scene regressed to a point where the height of vogue was wearing a sack with the most creative hole cut out for one's head. The term 'threadbare' became generous, as clothes in Hulumar were now so worn they could have doubled as spider webs.

As for heating their homes, the Hulumese found themselves in a conundrum. Camel chips, the fuel of the masses, had become as rare as a clean-shaven yak. The camels, once considered reliable producers of milk and biodegradable fuel pellets, had been recruited as star attractions at the circuses. As such, they were now far too busy balancing on balls and painting abstract art with their surprisingly dexterous lips to contribute to Hulumar's energy needs.

Winter approached with the subtlety of an elephant tap-dancing in a China shop. The Hulumese, bundled up in their chic potato sacks, huddled together, hoping to find warmth. Their tents, now colder than a snowman's handshake, were so devoid of heat that one could see one's breath at all times, leading to a brief and peculiar fashion of breath-shape competitions—though this fad faded with the realization that one can only admire so many cloud-like dragons and horses before yearning for a touch of actual warmth.

In the tents, families huddled together, reminiscing about the good old days of roasted lamb and loaves of bread as they chewed on the latest circus snack—popcorn flavored with the zesty tang of disillusionment.

The circuses, stubbornly impervious to the plight of economics or common sense, carried on. But the clowns' makeup could not mask the growing hunger in their eyes, and the acrobats performed with the listlessness of a cat on a hot afternoon—impressive but decidedly less energetic.

"Remember when we could afford almonds?" became the nostalgic sigh of the elders, who spoke of the War of the

Almonds as if it were a bedtime story filled with epic feasts and heroic snacks.

Jesters joked about the shortages, spinning satirical tales of farmers growing crops of dust bunnies and blacksmiths forging relationships because they, indeed, weren't producing anything else. But even their laughter was tinged with a chill, the kind that's not dismissed by mere snorts or giggles.

During these times, the Hulumese found their ingenuity kicking in, spurred by necessity. Recipes appeared for "Imaginary Stew" and "Wishful Thinking Pie." Fashion shows featured ensembles that were 'minimalist' out of necessity rather than aesthetic. As they sat, huddling for warmth and contemplating the circuses that had become both their joy and their downfall, the Hulumese couldn't help but wonder if the final act of this comedic tragedy was just around the corner.

Recipes From The Hulumese Kitchen
For Times of Plenty

Gilded Lamb with Almond Crust

Submitted by Chef Almondo Gourmette, Renowned Hulumar Culinary Expert

Ingredients:
- ❖ A rack of lamb, as tender as a Hulumese love song
- ❖ A handful of almonds, the spoils of a war once fought

❖ Fresh herbs from the gardens of Hulumar, kissed by the morning sun

❖ Salt and pepper, to taste

❖ Edible gold leaf, because why have plain when you can have gold?

Instructions:

Heat your oven to Hulumese victory feast levels.

Crush the almonds from the war-starting trees, blend them with chopped herbs, salt, and pepper, and make a crust as rich as Hulumar's history.

Push this mixture onto the tender rack of lamb like you're crowning the king of feasts. Then, roast the lamb to perfection, infusing the air with the scent of abundant fields and pleasant times.

Cover the lamb with the best edible gold leaf.

Serve this majestic dish with a side of storytelling, where each slice is a reminder of the wealth and power of a land that has known both the bitterness of War and the sweetness of peace.

The Legendary Hulumese Air Sandwich

*The Hulumese Air Sandwich is a culinary masterpiece born from the
imaginative Hulumar kitchens during the lean times.*

Ingredients

- 2 slices of hope (thinly sliced)
- A generous spread of patience
- A dash of Daydreams
- A pinch of laughter (for seasoning)
- Optional: A leaf of optimism (for garnish)
- Utensils: 1 Imaginary Panini Press & 1 Pair of rose-tinted glasses (for best viewing results)

Instructions:

Begin by laying out two slices of hope on your preparation
surface. Hope is best served fresh, so ensure it's sourced
from your morning aspirations.

Now, spread a generous layer of patience on each slice of
hope. Remember, patience is quite invisible, so spread it until
you feel it's just about enough to hold your sandwich
together through thick and thin.

Carefully sprinkle a dash of Daydreams over the bottom slice
of hope. These are calorie-free and add that essential 'je ne
sais quoi' (French, literally, 'I know not what') to the overall
flavor profile.

Season with a pinch of laughter. This adds light to the sandwich, essential for the perfect Hulumese Air Sandwich experience.

Press the two slices of hope together. Now, place your sandwich in the Imaginary Panini Press and pretend to cook until golden brown. The cooking time may vary depending on the strength of your imagination.

If you've chosen to include the optional leaf of optimism, now is the time to place it atop your sandwich for that artfully extra crunch.

Serve immediately, preferably on a sun-drenched windowsill with a view of the Hulumar markets coming back to life.

Enjoy your Air Sandwich with a side of satisfaction, knowing that no matter how bare the pantry, the Hulumese spirit remains ever nourished.

This sandwich pairs excellently with a tall glass of reflection and is best consumed in the company of good, similarly hungry friends. Enjoy your Hulumese Air Sandwich, a meal guaranteed not to weigh you down!

Chapter 8
The Lawmakers Raised Taxes
AGAIN and AGAIN

As the situation in Hulumar continued to deteriorate, the prices of everything from a loaf of almond bread to a second-hand sandal began to rise like a hot air balloon with a one-way ticket to the stratosphere. The economy was inflating faster than the ego of a cat who had just learned how to open the fridge.

In their infinite wisdom and experience in the delicate art of 'making things worse,' the Lawmakers saw the soaring prices and said, "I bet we could jump on that trend." Thus, they raised the taxes with the enthusiasm of a baker adding yeast to the dough, blissfully unaware that too much would soon make it all go 'pop.'

With a tax rate that climbed like an enthusiastic vine, citizens worked two jobs just to afford the tax on their first one. The tax on bread was so steep that people started to consider whether they might actually have to eat their money for sustenance, which, admittedly, still tasted better than the "air sandwiches" they had been forced to invent.

The Hulumese, ever resourceful, began using their tax statements as wallpaper. It was a decor choice that really spoke to the times—a kind of fiscal fresco that showcased the numbers going up and up, providing a fantastic visual aid for anyone explaining the concept of 'astronomical' to their children.

The Lawmakers, who had by now earned degrees in the School of Unintended Consequences, were stumped. "How could our plan of doing the same thing repeatedly possibly fail?" they pondered in their luxurious chambers while sipping on the costly wine they had taxed into exclusivity.

In their grand hall, they gathered around a giant abacus, which they had recently declared the National Calculator, and started sliding the beads back and forth in a manner they hoped appeared thoughtful and leader-like. "We need to tax those also!" exclaimed one Lawmaker, pointing at a bead that looked particularly shiny.

"And what shall we tax next?" another would ask, rubbing his chin to stimulate what he assumed was the universal gesture for conjuring wisdom. "Air? Dreams? The number of times a person blinks in a day?" The suggestions were many and varied, but all had one thing in common— they were ridiculous.

The new taxes were inventive, to say the least. There was the 'Looking at the Sky Tax' for those who dared to search the heavens for solace. The 'Walking on the Road Tax' was another creative way to encourage exercise by taxing those who chose not to sit at home on their tax-subsidized hassocks. And who could forget the 'Tax for Having Previously Paid Taxes,' a tax on top of other taxes that was as hard to understand as it was costly?

The Hulumese, however, were not to be outdone in their creativity. They started trading in favors, bartering, and the occasional IOU, which, unlike the official currency, did not require a wheelbarrow to carry enough for a loaf of bread. And speaking of bread, one beacon of common sense stood: Betsy the Baker. Amidst the chaos, her bakery remained a hub of practical wisdom and freshly baked resolve. With her hands as adept at shaping dough as they were at cutting through the town's growing nonsense, Betsy often voiced her concerns. 'Too much tax and not enough wheat make for a thin loaf,' she'd say, her words as crisp as her renowned crusty bread. Despite the madness swirling around, her bakery was a little haven where the scent of almond bread wafted stronger than the scent of discontent.

And so it went, the circle of financial folly continuing to spin. As prices increased, taxes also went up following the increase in prices. The lawmakers rode the wheel like hamsters with delusions of grandeur, blissfully unaware that the wheel was not, in fact, attached to anything and, indeed, wasn't powering the progress they imagined.

Amid rising taxes and the collective groan of Hulumar, the underground economy boomed, mainly because it was not actually underground but rather right in front of the lawmakers who were too busy inventing new taxes to notice.

Recipes From The Hulumese Kitchen
Bare Pantry Recipes

Patties of Potential

❖ Mash together the last legumes and the breadcrumbs of yesteryear's loaves.

❖ Form into patties representing the circular nature of fortune.

❖ Fry on a hot stone, using the heat of a community's united front.

❖ Echo of the Orchard Fruit Compote

❖ Gather the fallen fruits that still echo the abundance of the orchards.

❖ Stew them in their own juices over a flame of enduring hope.

❖ Sweeten with the nectar of resilience and a dollop of future dreams.

Twice-Sighed Beans

❖ Find the last beans in the pantry.

❖ Sigh once because that's all there is.

❖ Soak them overnight in tears of nostalgia for past feasts.

❖ Sigh again and cook them over a low whisper of hope.

Chapter 9
Misery and Gloom Replaced Joy and Pride

The atmosphere had taken a turn for the dismal in the once merry Land of Hulumar, where joy bubbled up like a fountain at a wine festival. Misery and gloom had set up shop where joy and pride once did a brisk trade, and business was, unfortunately, booming.

The general mood was comparable to the collective dismay you'd expect to find in a village of sunbathing turtles suddenly caught in a downpour. The populace moped around with the enthusiasm of overcooked noodles. Even the local composers, once the purveyors of catchy tavern tunes, were now singing ballads so woeful that onions cried when they heard them.

The town crier yelled out the news, again. This fellow had cried out so many new tax proclamations lately that he'd developed an exceptionally mournful wail, perfected by the somber realization that he, too, would have to pay the taxes he so artistically announced.

Parents tried to maintain a semblance of cheer at home, concocting fairy tales where the heroes were accountants who fought dragons named 'Inflation' and 'Taxation' with weapons forged in the fires of 'Audit' and 'Deduction.' These stories were meant to inspire, but they often ended with the children asking if they could learn this magical art of 'tax accounting,' too.

The once-proud Hulumese workers who had tirelessly tilled, toiled, and tailored now found their only solace in sarcasm. "Going to the market to not buy almond bread again," they'd say with a mirthless chuckle. "Maybe I'll splurge and not buy some cheese while I'm at it."

As for the circuses, they still drew crowds, but the laughter was hollow. Clowns' pies thrown in faces seemed an extravagant waste, and the acrobats' leaps and bounds reminded everyone just how far their currency had fallen. Even the strongmen were reduced to flexing their fiscal frugality by lifting nothing heavier than their lightened wallets.

And the lawmakers? Well, they wandered the marble halls of legislation, seemingly oblivious to the forlorn pall that had settled over Hulumar. They were the type of people who could walk through a rainstorm and marvel at how everyone else managed to get so wet. Misery, it seemed, had not found their door. Or perhaps it had, and they levied a tax on it, which made it go away and look for places where financial matters were handled more sensibly.

In this new Hulumar, where smiles were as scarce as hen's teeth, and optimism was now a collector's item, the Hulumese found solace in humor as dry as their fields and wit as sharp as the edge of a tax collector's ledger. The only thing left untaxed was laughter, and they clung to it like sailors to a life raft, hoping for rescue or at least a break in the clouds of their overcast economic landscape.

Recipes From The Hulumese Kitchen
Bare Pantry Recipes

Stone Soup Hulumar Style

Ingredients:
- 1 clean, smooth river rock (symbolic use only, not to be consumed)
- Water, enough to fill a large pot
- Any vegetables, bits of meat, or bones (scraps or peelings will do)
- A pinch of salt (or tears of laughter, for seasoning)
- A sprinkling of hope (essential)

Instructions:
Place the river rock ceremoniously in the center of a large pot. Admire its resilience as a metaphor for the Hulumese spirit. Then fill the pot with water and bring it to a simmer as you dream of better days.

As the water warms, gather any available vegetables, herbs, bones, or meat scraps and add them to the pot. Even the humblest of ingredients can contribute to this community feast.

Let the soup simmer as you season with a pinch of salt. Share stories of abundance with a few tears of happiness as the aroma fills the air.

When the ingredients are tender, remove the rock (do not attempt to eat it - this is where the line between culinary arts and geology is drawn).

Serve the soup with a sprinkling of hope, knowing that the rock in the pot helped stir the community's spirit.

Whispering Wheat Grass Soup

* Harvest the slender shoots of wheatgrass that have escaped the foragers' eyes.
* Simmer in a broth of dew collected at dawn and whispers of past harvests.
* Season with a pinch of optimism and serve with croutons of hardened resolve.

Chapter 10
When the Almonds Hit the Fan

In the once jovial Land of Hulumar, where laughter used to flow like the finest wine at a harvest festival, the mood had soured like milk left in the sun. Tired of their misery and gloom, the people were simmering like a pot about to boil over. It was a matter of time before the almonds hit the fan.

It all started one fateful morning when the town crier, whose voice had developed a high-pitch hoarseness, announced yet another tax. This time, it was a tax on sighing! The people had had enough. "We're being taxed for breathing out now?" they muttered. "What's next, a tax on blinking?"

An impromptu meeting was convened in the town square (since announced meetings had, of course, been taxed), and it resembled less a typical assembly and more a scene from 'The Hulumar Huddle of Discontentment.'

The air was charged with a kind of tension usually seen just before the climax of a comedy show's pie-throwing contest, all while children scampered around, playfully dodging the adults and scavenging for pie scraps.

Then, a figure emerged from the crowd, none other than Betsy the Baker, whose bread was as hard as the times they lived in. She climbed onto a barrel and declared, "Enough is enough!"

Betsy the Baker, known throughout Hulumar for her indomitable spirit (as much as her rock-hard bread), was a middle-aged widow of fiery determination and sharp wit that could slice through nonsense quicker than a hot knife through butter. With a laugh as hearty as her signature rye loaves and her hands, always dusted with flour, she was as capable of kneading dough as they were at rallying the disheartened villagers. Betsy had a knack for seeing the yeast of truth in the most convoluted of situations. Betsy's bakery was not just a source of (questionably edible) sustenance but also the go-to spot for a hearty dose of gossip, community chatter, and debates so spirited they could make her yeast rise in protest.

"It's time to knead this situation like dough and bake a better future!" Betsy declared.

Cheers erupted. Plans were hatched faster than chickens in an enchanted coop. The villagers decided to march up to the castle and demand that the king clean up the mess. "We want bread, not clowns!" they chanted, a slogan that was catchy, if not entirely rhythmical.

The procession to the castle struck a peculiar balance between a solemn demonstration and an accidental comedy show. It was less of a determined march (from lack of eating) and more of an impromptu parade of desperation. Children enthusiastically waved loaves of bread so hard they could double as makeshift clubs. At the same time, a group of Almond Farmers, brandishing old, lifeless almond branches, looked like they were auditioning for a role in 'The Ghosts of Harvests Past.' The whole scene had a touch of earnest resolve mixed with the kind of absurdity that makes you wonder if life had suddenly turned into a satirical play.

Upon reaching the castle, they were met by Sire B, the Not-So-Bright-But-Well-Meaning, who looked as if he'd just been told his crown was made of fool's gold. "Good subjects, what brings you to my humble—"

"We're here to un-juggle this mess you've created with the circuses and taxes!" interrupted Betsy, brandishing a loaf like a sword.

The king blinked, the gears in his head creaking like a rusty gate, while his eyes lingered on Betsy with a mix of apprehension and an unmistakable twinkle of admiration. "Ah, I see. Well then, perhaps we could discuss this over tea?" he suggested, his voice wavering slightly, revealing that he found the prospect of facing an angry Betsy more daunting, yet strangely more appealing, than confronting a fire-breathing dragon.

But it was too late for tea. The people demanded action, not scones. Reluctantly, Sire agreed to reverse the ridiculous taxes and replace the lawmakers with a council of wise villagers, including Betsy, who vowed to bring a 'bun' of common sense to the table.

Recipes From The Hulumese Kitchen
Bare Pantry Recipes

Imaginary Stone Stew

❖ Gather various stones and pretend they're exotic vegetables.

❖ Boil them in water seasoned with dreams of better days.

❖ Serve with a side of make-believe mashed tubers.

Grilled Dreams on a Stick

❖ Skewer your aspirations with bamboo sticks repurposed from abandoned garden trellises.

❖ Grill over the embers of a once roaring trade fire.

❖ Baste with the sauce of perseverance and garnish with sprigs of undying desire.

Chapter 11
The Lawmakers Face Their Comeuppance

In the once lively corridors of Hulumar's government, decisions had previously been tossed around as carelessly as a juggler at a festival. But now, the tables had dramatically turned, and the three lawmakers – Sir Huffenpuff, Lady Fancifull, and Lord Twiddlethumb – who once reveled in their tax-raising antics, found themselves in a pickle more sour than any they had previously fermented and as uncomfortable as sitting on a cactus but far less prickly and much more public.

Sir Huffenpuff, once known for inflating taxes as quickly as he inflated his chest, now faced a rather deflated reality: the deflation of his fortune. To his beloved public, whom he had previously viewed as little piggy banks on legs, he was now as popular as a skunk at a garden party or as a swarm of bees at a picnic. He'd strutted about, proposing tax hikes with the zeal of a bard singing off-key in the dead of night. But, when the granaries emptied and the looms fell silent, the people of Hulumar looked upon him with disdain that could sour milk. In a twist of poetic justice and to escape the ire of the citizens, Huffenpuff disguised himself as a traveling minstrel, singing for his supper and serenading for scraps, which were often more meager than the tax revenues he had once so merrily squandered.

Lady Fancifull, the cunning mind and architect of plush hassocks for all, was sure that soft hassocks and tumbling jesters were the keys to paradise. However, when the public funds ran dry, the hassocks were repossessed. Lady Fancifull found herself perched upon the unforgiving ground of reality. The same folks who had once lounged upon her hand-woven hassocks watching clowns and acrobats on a slippery tightrope now pointed fingers, forcing her to trade her "Lady" title for toil and swap silken pillows for burlap sacks in the marketplace she had neglected. Robes of responsibility replaced her lavish gowns; even worse, her days of sipping exotic teas were gone.

Lord Twiddlethumb was the free circuses mastermind who believed bread and games could placate a populace better than actual bread on tables and jobs in the market. Lord Twiddlethumb had twiddled the kingdom's finances into a tangle, but his days of twiddling his beard and thumbs were over. His fortunes evaporated like morning mist in the desert when the economy tumbled, much like a poorly baked almond cookie. Stripped of his silks and finery, Lord Twiddlethumb was condemned to work in the very fields he had allowed to fall unplanted. There, day by day, he learned the value of a hard day's work and the high cost of frivolity, his hands growing calloused as he now fiddled with his beard and pulled scraps out to feed his pet ants.

The legacy of Sir Huffenpuff, Lady Fancifull, and Lord Twiddlethumb was a stark reminder forever etched in the annals of Hulumar that those who govern must do so with foresight and prudence, for the consequences of their actions ripple through the ages, long after the last circus tent has been folded and the final tax collected.

Ultimately, no chains or dungeons were needed for these lawmakers; their captivity was in the reality they had created, their penance to be paid in sweat and humility.

The Hulumese couldn't help but chuckle at the sight — after all, it's not every day you see high-and-mighty lawmakers brought down to earth, landing with a thud as soft as a bag of tax receipts.

Now, led by the pragmatic wisdom of Betsy the Baker and her 'Almond Flour Advisory Alliance,' Hulumar embarked on its path to recovery. Laughter returned to its streets, not at the expense of clowns or jesters, but at the memory of how they'd all come together to reclaim their land from the absurdity of it all.

The story of the Great Uprising grew with each retelling. Each iteration was embroidered with more humor and hyperbole. The annals of Hulumar's history stood as a testament to the power of the people, a reminder that the true essence of society's prosperity lies not in the hands of a few but in the collective effort and resolve of its many.

Recipes From The Hulumese Kitchen
Bare Pantry Recipes

Wishful Thinking Pie

Ingredients:

- 1 cup of optimism, freshly harvested
- A handful of daydreams, ideally picked at the peak of whimsy
- A sprinkle of moonbeams for sweetness
- 3 spoonfuls of echoes from laughter-filled feasts
- A dusting of stardust (optional, for extra sparkle)
- The crust of determination rolled out thinly with a rolling pin of perseverance.
- A glaze of hope warmed to the temperature of a heart's yearning
- Utensils: 1 imaginary pie dish infused with memories of better days & 1 pair of rose-colored glasses to see the final product in its best light

Instructions:

Begin by preheating your dreams to the ideal future you envision.

Mix your optimism and daydreams in the bowl of aspirations until they form a thick paste of possibility.

Gently fold in the moonbeams, making sure not to overmix as they tend to dissipate if handled too roughly. This will add a natural sweetness to your pie, reminding you of the taste of success and honeyed almonds.

Now, pour the mixture into your imaginary pie dish – blink twice and remember that in Hulumar, imagination is the mother of invention.

Roll out your crust of determination on a flat surface of unshakable faith using a rolling pin of perseverance. Drape it over your pie, tucking in the edges with the finesse of a Hulumese tailor on better days.

For the glaze, take your hope and warm it gently with the fires of your passion and ambition. Brush it liberally over the top of the pie, giving it a sheen that says, "Everything is going to be okay."

Place the pie in the oven of anticipation and bake until the aroma of potential fills the room. Remembering the good old days takes as long as it takes.

Once baked, remove the pie from the oven of anticipation and let it cool on the windowsill of patience. Dust with stardust if you want that extra zing of cosmic wonder.

Serve generous slices of your Wishful Thinking Pie at a table set with laughter, good conversation, and a centerpiece of cherished memories.

Enjoy your Wishful Thinking Pie, best savored with a tall drink of resilience and a spoonful of humor. Remember, in Hulumar, the satisfaction is real even when the pie is imaginary!

Chapter 12
"Give Me A Solution"

In the grand halls of Hulumar, where decisions once echoed with solemn authority or as freely as the wine at a royal banquet, Sire Bumblebert, the Well-Meaning, paced with a furrowed brow, his shoulders sagging like the national morale. Sire Bumblebert still had his wits about him — albeit a bit windblown and with a few new grey hairs, making him look more like a wise wizard than the ruler of a somewhat topsy-turvy kingdom.

"We need a solution," Sire B muttered, his voice echoing with a blend of desperation and hope. Sire B glanced at his personal advisors, a group of stern-faced men and women whose brows were furrowed deep enough to plant almond seeds and who resembled a collection of statues more than a council of guidance.

The kingdom was tangled, like a yarn ball after a kitten party.

The advisors shuffled papers, cleared throats, and exchanged nervous glances, each silently praying for inspiration to strike - or at least for the person next to them to speak up first. But no words were forthcoming. It was as if wisdom had packed its bags and left Hulumar, leaving behind only empty platitudes.

The advisors, masters of ponderous thought and lengthy silence, offered nothing new. They were as effective as a one-legged man in a hopscotch tournament. Then, Betsy the Baker, known for her wisdom and sharp tongue (rumored to be as effective as her bread knife), stepped into the chamber.

Sire B, his eyes lighting up at the sight of her, replied, "Ah, Betsy, your wisdom is as welcome as a loaf of fresh bread in a famine. What do you suggest?"

Standing firm amidst the sea of advisors, Betsy said, "It's clear as the nose on your royal face that these endless taxes and circuses aren't the answer. You need advice that's grounded in something sturdier than flour and sugar. I say, seek the Wise Man of the Mountain. He has more wisdom in his pinky than we have in this whole room, and his counsel is as solid as my oldest rolling pin!"

"Indeed," Sire B mumbled, his gaze lost in the tapestries that depicted the War of the Almonds—untroubled days when the most significant concern was an errant nut allergy.

The room fell silent, the suggestion hanging like the aroma of Betsy's famous almond pastries. Sire B's expression shifted from intrigue to realization. "The Wise Man of the Mountain, of course! His insight might be the very ingredient we need."

The advisers exchanged glances, a silent ballet of bureaucratic bewilderment. "But Sire, that's as clear as mud after a landslide!" protested the advisors, "What can a hermit on a mountain offer that we, with all our collective wisdom, cannot?" they muttered indignantly.

Sire turned, a mischievous grin spreading across his face, "Ah, but dear advisors, have any of you ever managed to herd mountain goats and brew a decent herbal tea simultaneously? Sometimes wisdom isn't just in books and scrolls; it's in knowing when to listen to the wind and when to ask a goat for advice!"

Sire B, his gaze lingering on Betsy with a mix of admiration and something a little more tender, offered a hopeful smile. "Ah, Betsy, perhaps you can knead some sense into our dough of deliberation?"

Betsy, not one to shy away from a challenge or a chance to spar with royalty, retorted, "Sire if sense were butter, this council wouldn't be able to grease a pan. What you need is less fluff and more substance."

Tired of the same old counsel leading to the same old problems, Sire B considered Betsy's words and felt a spark of hope. After all, in a land where up had become down and left had become right, perhaps this advice was worth more than a bag of gold – or at least more than the current economic advice. "Very well," he announced, standing up with renewed vigor. "Prepare my horse! We shall seek the wisdom and counsel of the mountain sage that lies beyond these walls. Betsy, my kingdom is in your debt."

With a nod, Sire B turned to leave, his steps now purposeful. The advisors exchanged glances, a mixture of relief and apprehension in their eyes. As for Betsy, she returned to her bakery, her mind already whirring with plans for the kingdom's revival. She knew well that the future of Hulumar might just depend on the wisdom found at the mountain's peak and on a king willing to trek through the snow for his people.

Thus, Sire Bumblebert embarked on his journey, seeking answers and a path to lead Hulumar back to prosperity and joy. And as he left, the palace halls seemed a little brighter, filled with the faintest scent of hope and freshly baked bread.

The journey was not for the faint-hearted. The mountain paths were as twisted as the kingdom's current financial policies. But Sire pressed on, determined and surprisingly spry for a man usually confined to a throne.

Finally, after a trek that felt longer than a winter in Hulumar, Sire reached the mountain's peak.

In a cave adorned with nothing but wisdom and age and as sparsely decorated as a minimalist's dream home sat the Wise Man of the Mountain. He was surrounded by nothing but the echoes of his thoughts and the occasional visiting bat. He perched like an ancient owl, his beard so long it seemed to weave its own tales, having witnessed the passage of countless seasons from its cascading tendrils, which resembled waterfalls and vines.

As Sire entered the cave, draped in his royal ceremonial dress, which now seemed excessively heavy for mountain wear, the hermit-like Wise Man of the Mountain glanced up and dryly remarked, "Well, it's not every day that royalty stumbles into my humble abode. Did the palace run out of wise men, or have you come to discuss the weather?

Recipes From The Hulumese Kitchen
Bare Pantry Recipes

Rock Petroglyph Bread

Ingredients:
- Rocks with natural depressions or hollows (again, not for consumption, purely for the baking process)
- Any grains or ground roots available and mix with water, just enough to create a dough
- Place the rock near the edge of a fire
- A dash of imagination

Instructions:
Find a rock with a natural depression suitable for forming a flatbread. This will be your ancient Hulumese non-stick pan.

Mix whatever grains or ground roots you have with water to form a rudimentary dough. Then, pat the dough into the rock's hollow. It should resemble a flatbread, even if it dreams of being a cake.

Place the rock near the edge of a fire, close enough to feel the warmth but far enough to avoid turning your bread into charcoal. Once the bread is cooked, peel it off the rock.

Serve the bread with imaginative stories of the old days when rocks were just rocks and not an integral part of Hulumese cuisine, for in the Land of Hulumar, even the stones tell tales of survival and remind the people that resilience is the most crucial ingredient in any recipe.

Chapter 13
The Wise Man of the Mountain Speaks

In the heart of the cave, where shadows danced like elusive truths, the Wise Man of the Mountain peered at Sire Bumblebert through the thicket of his beard. He listened intently as Sire B recounted the tale of Hulumar's fall from grace, a narrative woven with taxes and circuses, like a peculiar tapestry of financial folly.

"My dear Sire," began the Wise Man, his voice echoing off the ancient walls, "your kingdom's tale is more tangled than my beard on a windy day. You see, in your noble quest to upholster every bottom in Hulumar, you've managed to unravel the very fabric of your society." (Even the Wise Man had heard about the hand-woven hassocks.)

He leaned forward, a twinkle in his eye. "Let me paint you a picture, Sire. Imagine Hulumar as a grand banquet. In your generosity, you invited everyone to feast without lifting a finger. But here's the twist — the food wasn't free. The sweat of a few simply paid for it while the many feasted."

The Wise Man chuckled, sounding like boulders in a gentle tumble. "You see, when you give people circuses and lavish comfort, funded by the toil of their neighbors, you create a kingdom of spectators, not participants. A land where idleness is king and work, the forgotten pauper."

Sire B listened, his expression a mix of enlightenment and the dawning horror of hindsight.

"Your citizens, once proud artisans and nut farmers, became connoisseurs of leisure. Why sow seeds when you can watch clowns? Why forge steel when you can recline on plush cushions and soft hassocks? You turned your kingdom into a grand theater, where the price of admission was the future."

The Wise Man's gaze sharpened. "What you've created Sire, is a feast of consequences, served cold by the chilling hand of reality. When everyone is invited to eat, but no one is cooking, the kitchen soon runs out of food."

He paused, allowing the metaphorical stew of his words to simmer in Sire's mind.

"Now, let's talk about these circuses," he continued. "A circus, my dear Sire, should be a place of wonder, not a crutch for society. You've made clowns and jugglers more vital than breadwinners. In a world dominated by entertainment, being serious is often considered foolish."

As the Wise Man spoke, the cave seemed to close in as if emphasizing the gravity of his words.

"In your effort to fill every plate, you've emptied the granary of initiative. You've stripped the loom of purpose in your desire to clothe every back. And in your race to entertain, you've benched the players of progress."

He leaned back, his beard settling down like the calm after a storm of profound thoughts. "Now, Sire, it's time to rewrite the menu of Hulumar. To cook a new future, you must first light the fire of industry and stoke the flames of self-reliance. Your people must learn to fish, not just eat the fish others catch. And just like cultivating almonds, they must understand that the sweetest fruits come from seeds of effort and care they plant themselves."

The Wise Man's eyes glinted with the final slice of wisdom. "Remember, Sire, TANSTAAFL – There Ain't No Such Thing As A Free Lunch. It's time for Hulumar to learn that the true feast is where every hand contributes to the meal and that money doesn't grow on almond trees."

With these words, the cave fell silent, save for the whisper of ancient truths lingering in the air, a recipe for redemption waiting to be followed.

Sire B the Well-Meaning descended the mountain with the careful steps one uses when trying not to start an avalanche or, in his case, a revolt against the sudden absence of freebies. "TANSTAAFL," he whispered with each step, which sounded suspiciously like a sneeze in the crisp mountain air. He was determined to turn his circus back into a kingdom, one earned lunch at a time.

Recipes From The Hulumese Kitchen
Bare Pantry Recipes

Cheese Wheel of Fortune

- ❖ Age cheese wheels in caves where the air is as rich as Hulumar's soil.
- ❖ Serve on platters carved from the trees of the once-forbidden luxury woodlands.
- ❖ Pair with a fig compote that hints at the sweetness of life.

Mirage Salad

- ❖ Pick a bouquet of wild greens that grow in the shadows of the granaries.
- ❖ Dress with an emulsion of mirage and memory: oil from yesterday's seeds, vinegar from the tartness of hard times.
- ❖ Sprinkle with seeds of hope found in the cracks of arid soil.

Chapter 14
TANSTAAFL

In the heart of Hulumar, the story of Sire Bumblebert's pilgrimage to the Wise Man of the Mountain spread like a sudden breeze before a storm. What wisdom had the Wise Man of the mountain yielded?

Sire B first met again with his advisers, who had perked up like sunflowers to the sun, their faces suddenly aglow, like lightbulbs – though due to energy conservation efforts, actual lightbulbs were now only a ceremonial fixture in the palace.

Sire B, addressing his advisors with a knowing look, said, "TANSTAAFL, my friends, means 'There Ain't No Such Thing As A Free Lunch.' It's a simple truth that every reward has its cost, and someone's effort must earn every benefit we enjoy

Upon hearing Sire B's explanation, the advisors exchanged glances before one of them, breaking into a grin, said, "Well, that explains why the palace kitchen keeps rejecting my IOUs for lunch! It's high time we roll our sleeves up and start earning our keep, one sandwich at a time!" Another, chuckling, added, "I suppose it's out with the free feasts and in with the 'bring your own bread' meetings!"

Sire Bumblebert, the Well-Meaning, felt a spark of hope, the kind that lights a fire in the belly of a leader facing the abyss. "Let us take the mountain man's wisdom to the people and sow the seeds for Hulumar's revival. We shall begin at dawn!"

The court erupted in applause; even the mime clapped in silent cheer as they all envisioned a kingdom restored—not by the lofty platitudes of a wise mountain hermit, but by the down-to-earth, dirt-under-the-fingernails hard work of its people, spurred on by a king who was ready to get his own royal hands a little dirty.

At dawn, Sire B the Well-Meaning was greeted with the enthusiasm reserved for tax collectors and those who bring soggy salads to picnics. "Hear ye! Hear ye!" he proclaimed, though most of his subjects were too busy sharpening pitchforks to notice. "The circuses are closed! It's time to get back to work!"

"People of Hulumar," he began, his tone a blend of humility and newfound resolve, "I sought the counsel of the Wise Man of the Mountain. His words were as simple as they were profound: 'TANSTAAFL' - 'There Ain't No Such Thing As A Free Lunch.'"

The people of Hulumar, aghast, looked up from their hassocks, their mouths agape, filled with the last of the free grapes. Murmurs rippled through the crowd. TANSTAAFL? This peculiar phrase was as intriguing as it was baffling. Was it a spell? A riddle? The latest dance move?

Just as the crowd's bewilderment grew, a familiar voice cut through the confusion. Betsy the Baker, her presence as commanding as ever, shouted from amidst the crowd, "What our Sire means, folks, is it's time we get our hands dirty again – for our bread, our crafts, and our pride!"

"But what about the less fortunate?" a humble farmer asked, his brow furrowing like a plowed field.

"Help them, certainly! But don't do the work for them. Give them seeds, not the fruit. Teach them to weave, to herd, to forge. Help them help themselves!" replied Sire B.

Hearts and minds in the crowd began to open, but Betsy's intervention turned the tide. "Work?" they echoed in unison as if the word was a relic from a bygone era, like 'VHS' or 'humility.'

Sire B continued, "For too long, we have lived under the illusion that life can be without effort, that prosperity falls like rain from the sky. But true prosperity, true happiness, is earned. We must work for our bread, nuts, comfort, and joy." (He meant to say almond nuts, of course.)

Standing tall among her fellow Hulumese, Betsy added, "That's right! Let's show our Sire we can do more than just clap at clowns. Let's rebuild Hulumar with our own two hands!"

Her words resonated, echoing Sire B's message with the clarity and relatability only she could provide. The crowd began to nod, a sense of purpose awakening within them.

Balancing precariously on a barrel, Lord Chuckles, The Royal Hulumar Court Jester, leaned over to a wide-eyed kid and quipped, 'Say goodbye to free munchies, my young friend. It's time to trade our forks for shovels!'

Indeed, as Sire's words sank in, a shift began. The farmers missed bragging about their prize-winning almonds and their bountiful harvests. The blacksmiths, remembering the ring of hammer on anvil, smiled. The weavers, dreaming of looms spinning with vibrant threads, felt finger twitches of excitement. They were simply thread over heels to be back at their looms.

As Sire B concluded, a newfound energy surged through the crowd. The phrase "TANSTAAFL" became a rallying cry, a mantra of rejuvenation. It was chanted in the fields, hummed in the workshops, and whispered in the homes.

And so, as the sun set on Hulumar that day, a new chapter began. The people, once asleep in a dream of endless leisure, awoke to the dawn of a new day, where each meal, stitch, and crafted tool was a testament to their resilience, spirit, and the wisdom of the wise man in the mountain. They had lost their way but found it again through a simple, powerful truth from the Wise Man in the mountain: TANSTAAFL, There Ain't No Such Thing As A Free Lunch.

And in the evenings, as the people gathered, tired yet fulfilled, they would share stories of the day's labor, laughing and saying, "TANSTAAFL, my friends. TANSTAAFL."

Recipes From The Hulumese Kitchen
Bare Pantry Recipes

Imaginary Stew

Ingredients:
- A pot full of potential
- Unlimited cups of creativity
- A large scoop of imagination
- Several pinches of pretend
- A generous pour of invisible ingredients
- A dollop of daydreams
- A sprinkle of make-believe spices
- A dash of diversion
- Hearty laughs to taste
- Utensils: 1 ladle of laughter & 1 serving spoon of spirit

Instructions:
Begin by placing your pot of potential on the stove of optimism, set to a medium glimmer of hope.

Stir in unlimited cups of creativity and imagination, allowing the blend to simmer with your wildest culinary fantasies and boundless possibility.

Now add several pinches of pretend. Close your eyes and imagine the scent of a feast fit for royalty.

Pour in your invisible ingredients, including intangible carrots, ethereal onions, and nonexistent potatoes. Each adds depth and body to the stew, visible only to the inner eye.

Mix in a dollop of daydreams. What are your heart's desires? A successful harvest? A full pantry? Let these dreams swirl into your creation.

Season with a sprinkle of phantom salt harvested from the tears of joy and pepper ground from the peppercorn tree in your mind's enchanted garden.

Add a dash of diversion. A joke, a giggle, or a silly dance around the kitchen can bring out your Imaginary Stew's flavors.

Let your stew simmer with hearty laughs. After all, laughter is the secret ingredient in all Hulumese cuisine.

Serve with a ladle of laughter and a spoon of spirit. Each bowl should be filled to the brim with cheerful banter and shared with friends who appreciate the fine art of invisible gastronomy.

There you have it, the classic Hulumese Imaginary Stew. Bon appétit, or as the Hulumese say, "Bon imagination!"

Chapter 15
A Plan of Action

A remarkable transformation unfolded in the land of Hulumar, much like a play where the third act reveals all the characters learned their lessons, only with fewer feathered hats and dramatic monologues.

Sire had a plan. A plan so audacious that it involved actual soil and sweat.

Firstly, he abolished the tax on hard work, which had previously been filed under 'Things Hulumese Loathe,' right between 'plagues' and 'unexpected visits from in-laws.' Instead, he introduced a novel concept: the less you worked, the more you paid. It was a reverse psychology of sorts, or reverse taxation, if you will.

Once they got over the shock of being allowed to keep their produce, the farmers returned to the fields, their plows carving the earth with renewed vigor. The shepherds, lured by the promise of keeping their wool, stopped trying to knit sweaters directly on the sheep and started shearing again.

Sire introduced 'Work Fairs,' where the Hulumese could show off their talents, from cheese-making to poetry about cheese-making, which was surprisingly a big hit. He replaced free circuses with free workshops, where you could learn to juggle but also to pickle vegetables, which was slightly less exciting but far more practical.

Slowly but surely, Hulumar regained its former glory, and its fields once again flourished with the almond trees that had been the kingdom's pride and the heart of their victorious War of the Almonds. The bountiful almond harvests, celebrated with festivals and feasts, became symbols of the resilience and rejuvenation of Hulumar.

The granaries filled up like the stomach of a king at a banquet, and the fields grew bountiful as if the earth itself was in a particularly generous mood.

The new motto of Hulumar became 'Work, Save, Prosper,' which didn't have quite the same ring as 'Free Lunches Here!' but it looked fabulous on a coin.

And what of the infamous trio – Sir Huffenpuff, Lady Fancifull, and Lord Twiddlethumb? Now humbled and wiser, they joined the communal dance of productivity. Seen occasionally with dirt under their nails or flour in their hair, they became symbols of the adage, "From great follies come great lessons."

The Almond Wars, now a story of the past, symbolized the lessons learned and the wisdom gained. As the almond trees blossomed each year, they stood as reminders of resilience, growth, and the sweet fruits of labor. The markets brimmed with goods, the fields swayed with crops, and genuine, heartfelt laughter filled the air. The Hulumese celebrated hard work, the joy of earning one's keep, the sweetness of a day's labor, and the beauty of a community united in purpose and pride.

And so, Hulumar thrived, a kingdom reborn from its own ashes, a tale of caution turned into a legend of resurgence. They worked, played, and lived – not as subjects of a well-meaning Sire but as architects of their own fate, authors of their own story, and the sculptors of a future as bright as the Hulumese sun.

Henceforth, Hulumar was not only a land of plenty but also a land of sensibility. And if occasionally someone yearned for the old days of circuses and free grapes, they only had to remember the long lines at the tax collector's booth to snap out of it.

As Hulumar bloomed anew, so too did an unexpected romance. Sire Bumblebert, previously known more for his good intentions than his romantic prowess, found himself utterly enchanted by Betsy the Baker's combination of wit, wisdom, the heavenly aroma of her bakery, and a tendency to bake pastries that could melt even the stoniest of royal hearts.

Their courtship was the talk of Hulumar, a blend of royal blunders and bakery banter that could have filled a book of its own. Betsy wooed the King with an array of delectable pastries, each a testament to her affection, while the King, usually more at home with royal decrees than romantic gestures, showered her with the kind of attention and admiration that would soften the hardest of sourdoughs. Once clumsy in matters of the heart, the King pursued Betsy with the same determination he approached state matters.

Amid a laughter-filled almond harvest festival, Sire Bumblebert, knee-deep in almond shells, blurted out to

Betsy, "Will you be the queen of my heart and the almond to my pie?" causing an uproar of giggles.

With a twinkle in her eye and a grin as wide as her famous almond tarts, Betsy replied, "Only if you promise our life will be as rich and nutty as these almonds, Sire. Yes, I'll marry you!"

Their eventual wedding held amidst the almond groves, was as delightful as it was unconventional – complete with a cake so tall, it needed its own royal decree to be cut. The people of Hulumar chuckled and cheered; their beloved Sire had finally found his Queen, and she, in turn, had found her King, proving that even in the most twisted of tales, love could rise like well-kneaded dough.

Sire B the Well-Meaning, now known as 'Sire the Sensible,' was lauded for his wisdom. He even allowed a statue erected in his honor, which he modestly requested to be life-sized and not a foot taller.

Sire Bumblebert would often stand on his balcony with Betsy, looking out over the almond farms, bustling marketplace, and the once-again prosperous kingdom, and chuckle. "TANSTAAFL," he'd say with a smile, a gentle reminder that the best lunch was earned by a good day's work.

And the Hulumese? They'd sneeze back respectfully, "TANSTAAFL, Sire. TANSTAAFL."

Chapter 16
Epilogue: The Almond Wars' Lasting Legacy

Happy endings, much like a perfectly baked almond cake, hold a cherished spot in the world of storytelling. They conclude our journey with the same satisfaction you get from that last bite of dessert, tying up all the loose ends with a comforting sense of wholeness. To witness a community we've grown fond of now find its path to peace, redemption, and joy, is heartwarming. It's like watching your clumsy puppy finally master the art of fetching. For Hulumar, their newfound success was about more than just accumulating wealth; it was a realization that went beyond their usual simple understanding.

In this tale, Hulumar emerges wealthier and with a rekindled spirit of industriousness, tinged with a dash of humor, like a chef who accidentally flips a pancake onto the ceiling. The community's new mantra, "TANSTAAFL" – There Ain't No Such Thing As A Free Lunch – becomes their guiding star and guiding principle. It served as a reminder that while happiness doesn't arrive ready-made, like a pizza delivery, putting in the effort to achieve it is always valuable.

But every story, especially one as layered as 'The Almond Wars,' comes with its own morals. It teaches us to be careful with the laws we enact, lest we end up like someone who's built a robot for house cleaning that accidentally throws out the furniture. For Hulumar, cleaning up the legislative mess was as glamorous as scrubbing pots after a feast, hardly a royal ball. This process humbled the kingdom's leaders, teaching them that with great power comes significant responsibility and, occasionally, an auditorium of angry citizens with pitchforks and questions.

This narrative was about more than Hulumar finding its way back to prosperity. It chronicled their shift from a gloomy state, brought on by excessive taxes and an unhealthy addiction to leisure, to a scene of productivity and heartfelt joy. It's like watching a garden bloom after a long, harsh winter. The story vividly captures the gradual change in the people's mindset and values, painting a picture of a community marching towards a brighter tomorrow.

Central to this transformation was the wake-up call faced by the lawmakers. Their path from slapstick mistakes to meaningful insights, and eventually, a revolution in how they ran the kingdom, mirrored Hulumar's own journey to recovery. Sire Bumblebert's personal transformation, spurred by his chat with the Wise Man of the Mountain, was crucial. Embracing the "TANSTAAFL" principle marked his evolution from a ruler to a true leader, one who listens not just to the wind but also to the whispers of the almond trees.

Hulumar's cultural and social shift was a study of adaptation. The community had to navigate significant changes in farming, craftsmanship, and trade, learning to balance welfare, work, and leisure. Hulumar's story celebrates rejuvenation – a kingdom thriving with a newly balanced approach to life.

As the final pages of this almond-scented saga turn, let's not forget the quirky characters who flavored our journey. Remember Betsy the Baker, with her flour-dusted apron and wisdom-infused loaves, who rose from local baker to Queen, mixing resilience with every batch of dough. Her partnership with Sire Bumblebert, once a king more akin to a befuddled baker than a shrewd monarch, blossomed into a union of hearts and minds, proving that even in a kingdom of oddities, love and understanding find fertile ground.

Nor should we overlook the comedic trio of lawmakers, whose high-flying ambitions and tax-raising follies served as a cautionary yeast, teaching us that the rise and fall of fortune can be as unpredictable as a soufflé in a storm. Their eventual humbling, much like over-kneaded dough, reminds us that the true strength of leadership lies in service and humility, not power and pride.

In Hulumar, where almonds once sparked wars and circuses spun fortunes, the true victory was in rediscovering the joy of simplicity – the art of nurturing an almond tree, the satisfaction of a day's honest work, and the warmth of a community knit tightly by shared struggles and triumphs.

In wrapping up this tale, we ponder the lessons the Hulumese learned. The importance of hard work, sustainable policies, and finding harmony in life's symphony are the themes that resonate. Like the almond trees that dot their landscape, these lessons stand tall, offering fruits of wisdom and knowledge for generations to come. Prosperity and joy aren't just about what's in the granary or the purse; they're about what's in the heart. The Hulumese, once lost in a circus of excess, found their way back through laughter, labor, and a newfound respect for the humble almond, which, much like their journey, is simple on the outside but rich and complex within.

So, let us toast to Hulumar, to its people, and its almonds, with the hope that its story, steeped in folly, wisdom, and a dash of nuttiness, serves as a reminder that sometimes, the most profound lessons are hidden in the most unexpected of shells. TANSTAAFL!

Recipes From The Hulumese Kitchen
Bare Pantry Recipes

Echo of the Orchard Fruit Compote

- ❖ Gather the fallen fruits that still echo the abundance of the orchards.
- ❖ Stew them in their own juices over a flame of enduring hope.
- ❖ Sweeten with the nectar of resilience and a dollop of future dreams.

The Hulumese Kitchen
A Culinary Adventure

In the enchanting land of Hulumar, where stories are as plentiful as almonds in autumn, the Hulumese Kitchen is a testament to culinary creativity. Here, cooking isn't just about feeding the body; it's a whimsical journey of feeding the soul, especially when the cupboard's as empty as the town crier's promise of quiet.

These recipes, a blend of resilience, ingenuity, and a pinch of humor, reflect the true spirit of Hulumar. From the hard times, when chefs became illusionists with their 'Imaginary Stew' and 'Wishful Thinking Pie,' to the prosperous days when every dish was a celebration as grand as the annual 'Almond Jubilee.'

Inventive use of non-ingredients was the name of the game when the pantry echoed like the village square at midnight. The Hulumese Kitchen is renowned for turning the bare minimum into a feast fit for royalty or at least for a very imaginative pauper. In their grand culinary improvisation tradition, the chefs mastered the art of making much ado about, well, practically nothing!

And let's not forget the classic use of rocks — an ingredient that wouldn't make the cut in any other kingdom's cookbook. In Hulumar, rocks in the pot symbolize resourcefulness and the sheer will to cook something out of anything. They were the zero-calorie, rustic surprise in every meal, perfect for the diet-conscious and the humor-loving. Just remember, as the Hulumese chefs often joked, it's best to fish out the rock before you set the table unless dental expenses are on the menu.

During times of prosperity, gold found its way into recipes, not just for the bling but as a symbol of transformation and triumph. Gold-leafed honey drizzler on freshly baked bread, anyone? It's a culinary nod to the times of struggle, a reminder that the sweetest victories are those hard-earned.

So, in the whimsical world of the Hulumese Kitchen, whether you're dishing out imaginary soups or feasting on gold-infused delights, remember that every meal tells a story. In Hulumar, where the almond trees whisper recipes to those who listen, cooking is an adventure, a celebration, and sometimes, a delightful act of defiance against the ordinary. Here, a meal is never just a meal – it's a chapter in the ongoing tale of a land where resilience, laughter, and a good dash of creativity are the most cherished ingredients.

Recipes From The Hulumese Kitchen
Bare Pantry Recipes

Wisp of Wheat Bread

- ❖ Collect the dust from empty granaries and knead with hope and a prayer.
- ❖ Let rise in the warmth of sunny expectations.
- ❖ Bake in an oven heated by collective ambition.

Faux Fowl

- ❖ Take a shadow of a passing bird (preferably a plump one).
- ❖ Marinate it in the idea of herbs and spices.
- ❖ Roast over a fire fueled by the memory of grand feasts.

Wind Pie

- ❖ Capture the essence of the wind by leaving a pie crust out on a breezy day.
- ❖ Fill with promises of tomorrow and the aroma of yesteryear's harvest.
- ❖ Decorate with petals of the rare bloom called resilience.

76

TANSTAAFL and
The War of the Almonds

The War of the Almonds is a parody, a fascinating narrative that humorously and insightfully explores the consequences of well-intentioned policies and the rediscovery of work ethics and sustainable prosperity.

The War of the Almonds is a loosely based parody on a short, unnamed article from Newsweek, 1975, that starts, 'After the War of the Almonds.' The author is unknown.

The 'TANSTAAFL' acronym and the article from Newsweek were read into the Congressional Record on Tuesday, May 20, 1975, by the Honorable William L. Armstrong, a Congressman from Colorado. (15566 – pg. 69 – 1975 Congressional Record)

"There ain't no such thing as a free lunch" first appeared in writing in the Columbia Law Review in 1945.

It is believed that Robert A. Heinlein was the first person known to publish the term "TANSTAAFL" in his book, "The Moon is a Harsh Mistress," published in 1966.

About the Author

The author of "**The War of the Almonds**," Brenda L. High, is not just a unique blend of historian, humorist, and culinary enthusiast but also a sly political satirist. While seemingly a whimsical journey through the world of nuts and gastronomic exploits, this book is a cleverly veiled political parody. Brenda cleverly weaves elements of contemporary politics into the fabric of Hulumar's almond-centric universe, delivering chuckles and profound insights with equal prowess.

This knack for political parody was perhaps honed during Brenda's stint as a juggler in a circus, where juggling objects was less challenging than juggling the eccentric personalities and politics backstage. Known in certain quirky literary circles as the 'Almond Whisperer,' Brenda masterfully uses the tale of "The Almond Wars" to poke fun at the absurdities of political systems, all under the guise of a battle for nutty dominance. When not engaged in deep conversations with almond trees (which are rumored to be excellent political analysts), Brenda can be found sipping almond milk lattes, always with a twinkle in her eye, hinting at the next political misadventure to befall the unsuspecting inhabitants of Hulumar...or?

Back cover reviews

"Being a professional jester, I know funny, and **'The War of the Almonds'** is hilarious! Brenda High has juggled history, humor, and almonds with the skill of a true comedic acrobat. It's a laugh-a-minute romp through Hulumar's past, and as someone who's seen his fair share of real court blunders, I can attest to its accuracy in capturing political silliness, though **I still think my metaphors are better."**

Lord Chuckles, The Royal Hulumar Court Jester

"Upon sampling **'The War of the Almonds'** by Brenda High, I was prepared for a recipe for disaster. Instead, **I found almond joy** in the author's ability to turn our beloved nut into a symbol of folly and triumph. My only critique? The book could use more almond-based recipes. Four out of five stars, with one star reserved for when she publishes 'The War of the Almonds Cookbook.'"

Chef Almondo Gourmette, Renowned Hulumar Culinary Expert

"As ruler of Sulumaze and victor of the real Almond Wars, I was amused to find myself chuckling at Brenda High's witty **'The War of the Almonds.'** While taking creative liberties, she amusingly recasts our triumph as a nutty, satirical romp. A royal thumbs up for the humor, though **let's not forget that Sulumaze was the true victor."**

- King Reginald the Victorious, Unchallenged Monarch of Sulumaze

"As a historian, I approached **'The War of the Almonds'** with academic skepticism. This book takes liberties with facts, yes, but it's a reminder that **sometimes history is told by those who can tell the funniest stories about it**."

Professor Scribble, an Esteemed Historian at the University of Hulumar

"Reading **'The War of the Almonds'** by Brenda High, **I braced for satire but got a whole sack of salt!** The portrayal of us lawmakers is as blown out of proportion as my great aunt's wig collection. Sure, I snickered – in sheer disbelief! The humor's as delicate as a clown at a funeral. This book is a far cry from the true elegance of Hulumar's history. Two stars, and that's me being generous."

Lady Fancifull, Keeper of Plush Hassocks, Former Lawmaker of Hulumar